TELEKINESIS

VICTIMS OF HIS HEAD
VOL. 1

DEVLEENA NAIK

Copyright © Devleena Naik 2024
All Rights Reserved.

ISBN 979-8-89475-257-0

This book has been published with all efforts taken to make the material error-free after the consent of the author. However, the author and the publisher do not assume and hereby disclaim any liability to any party for any loss, damage, or disruption caused by errors or omissions, whether such errors or omissions result from negligence, accident, or any other cause.

While every effort has been made to avoid any mistake or omission, this publication is being sold on the condition and understanding that neither the author nor the publishers or printers would be liable in any manner to any person by reason of any mistake or omission in this publication or for any action taken or omitted to be taken or advice rendered or accepted on the basis of this work. For any defect in printing or binding the publishers will be liable only to replace the defective copy by another copy of this work then available.

*This book contains sensitive subjects that may
trigger certain audiences, including graphic imagery,
violence, anxiety, suicide and assault.
Reader discretion is advised.*

ACKNOWLEDGEMENTS

I would deeply like to thank my parents (Mr. Madhusudan Naik and Mrs. Jemamani Naik) for giving me birth and also for the money I needed to publish this book. This whole acknowledgement section could have been an email, but my mum was probably way too curious to see her feature on the book, and she wasn't supposed to read it at all! The same applies to my Father, too!

My brother, my absolutely amazing friends and wonderful siblings, whom I must not name because I am sure that I will get myself into great trouble if I even dare miss a single one...

My Manager/boss, Mr Rajesh Gupta, for doing the most boss thing ever by giving me a strict timeline to finish this book when I told him that I couldn't do my job anymore since it did not give the thrill that I was seeking from my life...

And the most special mention to whoever told me, 'You should write a book about it!' when I told the person about this dream (It's probably you, Keya).

If we have ever crossed paths, know that you have played your part pretty well!

TABLE OF CONTENTS

CHAPTER 1
CATFIGHTS

"I know you love her more, Mum; you don't have to pretend to care, you know!"

And there goes yet another day. Is this even a wrestle anymore? All these kinds of probes are an uninteresting chore now. Lilac, my little sister, is beloved (so to say), and I call her Lil'ass! Suits the pain that she gives me! Mum and Dad would get vexed every time they'd hear me saying that! But did that ever stop me from doing it?

Hell NO!!

I know all the siblings have this shared aversion towards each other, but she? She is indistinguishable, and I can hardly stand her. Every time I try to act cool, she triggers the most delicate reigns in my head that make me want to kill her!! It's literally the same, starting with her doing something stupid, not letting me focus on anything, shaking her little ass all over the place and in front of me, playing the tackiest and utterly sexualised song on repeat day in and day out! How could someone not despise these 15-year-olds, as well as their whole generation? The moment I mutter a single word out of aggression, she complains, and Mum gets on top of me for being a bad sister and a spoilt daughter, leading to me being a disappointment in general. She gives her the perfect chance to make me question my life!

I am Mauve, an Art Honours Major in my sophomore year at the University of Artwear, and... I pretty much hate everyone around me. And why so? Cause I am a jerk. I must have gotten into a dozen fights in college already; consequentially, people around me hate me the same. I am not at all proud of this, but I guess this is what 'MCR' and 'Panic!' have done to me over the years.

Very few people keep me rational and lucid, but I hardly like being around anyone. Everyone has something to gain, and that's the sole reason why they approach you. None of them delight me enough to mean anything of value, and vice versa! This way, no one has anything to lose. That's me, nothing too much, nor too little.

6th June 2015

Mum: "You girls wake up at once or suffer the consequences if I come upstairs!"

Why not? It's the best way to start the morning. I hardly get any sleep; my insomnia keeps me up all night by changing positions. I had to pull an all-nighter because we had to submit a proposal for the upcoming project of a ridiculous subject to that so-called 'professor.' On top of that, my little sister has to keep talking all night on the phone. The novelty of listening to her conversations is officially over, especially when she discusses the same old things with each of her friends INDIVIDUALLY. I've memorised their entire stories now and can recite them verbatim, even in my sleep. I really hope that no one gets a younger sibling. My college starts at 9:30am, but I have to leave home at eight to arrive on time. On top of that, I have to wait for my sister to get out of the bathroom early, which she fails to do every day.

Mum: "I will be waiting no longer. Do you hear me?"

'Coming, Mum,' the monster is up to; here we go again...

I walk downstairs and put butter on the bread while she is in the washroom. I need to brush my teeth, take a bath, dress up, pack my bag, do a final review, finish the breakfast and leave! I'll be a dead corpse if I don't reach on time. Huff, I am already behind schedule!!! What on Earth is taking her so long?

* * *

She takes TWENTY MINUTES to come out of the washroom, not realising that she has threatened her life. She was literally shitting while playing Bruno Mars!!! Not even realising that I had been shouting at her to come out faster...

I dress myself in a drift to reach the breakfast table to grab my sandwich, but to my surprise (is this even surprising anymore?) It's that Lil'ass. She took my sandwich!!! I give her a grieved glare, she does what she can do best, play the cry-baby.

Mum: "Will the two of you stop? We don't have time to deal with your trivial arguments every single day. Here, I have breakfast for both of you. Lilac, you'll be in big trouble if you don't finish your milk without spilling it."

Lil'ass has some major issues with drinking milk. She either pretends to be late and leaves it or goes out and pours it into the garden. It's amusing to see what new thing she does every day to get rid of it! I grab my lunch and sit back for one final preview of the project. Lil'ass comes and sits next to me and starts scrolling through Instagram.

Does she have to do this right now? When I need to focus!! Like she loves to trigger me and she succeeds every time.

Lilac: "Why do you have to work on the breakfast table? You should have saved up your time and worked properly before."

She always makes me wonder where she gets the audacity to say such things.

"Are we really doing this? You were the one bitching about Sharya all night for wearing padded lingerie twice her cup size, acting like a 'pick-me' girl! Flirting with all your guy friends."

I saw the sudden change in expression on my Dad's face, which was of annoyance and discomfort. Of course, it's really shocking, I guess? She isn't your 5-year-old to not be talking about such stuff.

Mum: "What are you girls talking about on my breakfast table? Can we not have one single meal in peace? All I ever asked from you guys was to behave like sensible adults who at least know how to talk properly. Cut this crap at once! I don't want you both at the table for more than ten minutes now, so eat and dash off!"

My Mum has never failed to startle me, but I also think that it would be normal human behaviour, given we both shared the same space. I guess that is the price you pay if you wanna live rent-free.

Lil'ass attempted to grab the headphones from the back of the table without moving. She managed to grab them but accidentally spilt her glass of milk on my laptop! The keyboard's backlight turned off, and the screen froze. I quickly turned over my laptop and tried to remove the liquid. I removed the battery and used a towel to pat it dry, hoping that the liquid did not reach the motherboard. Despite my efforts, I couldn't get it to work. The keys stopped responding, and I was unable to fix it.

In short, I am doomed.

My hands were shaking uncontrollably as I realised there were only 3 hours left before the presentation, and I had no backup. The thought of his inevitable scolding for not submitting the work made my heart pound in my chest. A gnawing ache twisted in my belly, making it hard to focus. I struggled to catch my breath as sweat beaded on my forehead. His words echoed in my mind, striking fear into the depths of my conscience.

I felt overwhelmed by the suffocating horror of the situation, unable to bear it any longer.

"What have you done!?" I wasn't even feeling angry now, but helpless.

Lilac: "It was a mistake, I'm sorry!"

"Yes, you were. Tell me something I don't know," my words were unapologetic.

Mum: "Have you girls started again? Why are you shouting?"

She came to see the menace and understood at once by the horrors on my face.

Lilac: "Why do you talk to me like that? It's not like I wanted to ruin your project. I told you I am sorry. Tell me how I can help you to fix this!"

"You know what? You can help me by getting out of my life! I'll surely be happier that way!!! I cannot go to the class without this."

I couldn't bear the anxiety anymore, and I fell on the floor.

Mum: "You do not talk to your sister like that, old lady. We will help you fix this; no need to attend your class today. I will call your professor and talk to him, and you (looking at Lilac) go straight to your school. You better do something about your careless behaviour. I am not going to spare you from all your mistakes!"

[She grabs her backpack and dashes off. As Dad comes walking in...]

Dad: What is this chaos that you girls have created early in the morning!?

He glances at the laptop and then finds me on the floor sobbing. He ensures to get it fixed by the evening. Meanwhile, Mum insists on me getting some rest.

I was 18 years old when I had my first panic attack, and I know for a fact that I have to keep my calm in all possible scenarios because if I don't... I start hyperventilating, and as the doctor said, I even have chances of severe chest aches and an endless period of unconsciousness.

I have started to hate my sister more and more with each passing day. And she makes no effort to differ my disliking. I remember being super excited when Mum broke the news that I was going to be an older sister, but this was not what I expected! I was seven back then. Watching her smile, laugh, and utter the words 'mama' was all the joy in the world for us. She turned out to be this brilliant girl who memorised the table of thirteen when she was freaking four years old! Pretty much three years earlier than an average kid. I don't know if it was too great of a deal, but it was enough to impress the guests coming over. It was since then that she had been their trophy daughter. Smart, witty, absolutely pretty; Outspoken and intelligent kid. Pretty much the exact opposite of me. I am a lover of Arts and Philosophy and making real-life connections. I couldn't learn the textbook Math. But, guess what our parents loved more!? Yeah, the studious child! The sad part is, to them, her goals of being an astrophysicist seemed more ambitious than my endeavours of being a full-time commissioned artist and having my work put up in a museum.

My Mum works in the house the whole day and sells flowering plants online as her side hustle, and Dad works full-time as the HR manager for a huge finance company. It's with his money that we are even able to afford a lifestyle. But the loans and insurances keep us from spending for 'wants!' Dad never really pressured me for any career choice in particular, but in recent years, I have seen him growing hesitant about my life and whether the money he has saved for us would do any good! Mum had to give up on her education to raise us (All Hail Patriarchy)! But I am glad that she has gotten back to her feet and grown her own small business. As for Lil-ass, she would have been a great kid and an inspiration, had she not been my younger sister! She was the perfect daughter that my parents always wanted! And I am glad they had her in the first place.

It wasn't much after she turned five when she started scribbling on my textbooks, taking my toys particularly, and eventually breaking them, to throwing them away so that I don't see, she'd take all my stuff and ruin them!

I calmed myself from saying anything to her despite her being so annoying since she was immature and brainless for the longest time, until that one day...

My best friend, Io, lived in the neighbourhood. I could live in a world happily with no one but her... I always hoped Lil'ass would be like her and have the same vibe as mine. But she had to shift to a faraway city with her family. She gave me a beautiful diary as her parting gift that said the words, verbatim, "I know how you share every problem of your life with me; consider this a part of me and keep this safe as you did to me. I'll be with you even when I am not around..."

I was ten when she left; she was the only one I knew all my life! I wouldn't eat anything for two days and had fallen sick because of it. But I did as she said; I would write addressing her as a letter religiously every day. We were too young and could not exchange telegrams; back then, we just had one landline and a cell phone that Dad wouldn't let us use as it was strictly for work. We never heard back from them. I hoped to hear from her after they had settled wherever they were supposed to be...

5 years later, after my final exams in the ninth grade, we had to resell our old academic books. I had cleared my extra notebooks outside, and Dad was supposed to leave for the shop by midday. I kept my stuff in a carton and returned to clean the room back again, and Lilac was obviously late in doing her work. Mum started shouting from downstairs, which got her into a rush, and she accidentally packed my dairy.

Dad beautifully went and sold off the things.

Two days later, I turned to make my diary entry when I realised that it was missing. I whirled the whole house upside down to find it, screaming like a lunatic. I felt as if I would lose Io again. The only part of her that ever existed in me after she left was the diary, which was gone, and I didn't want to let that happen. My heart rate was triggered, and my chest felt heavy! I described to Father how it looked, and he confirmed to me that he could recall something of that sort kept in Lilac's box. I jumped on my bike and raced my way to the garage bookshop. Father saw my insanity and got out with the car to pick me up halfway! We reached the shop, but the owner said that they sold that day's load for recycling. They wouldn't even let me check their store one last time, as the only resort of my helplessness. My eyes had turned burning red as I returned home, straight to the bed. I did not talk to anyone that day again and cried myself to sleep.

...

The next day, Lilac came with a new diary for me and apologised for having sold mine. Mum insisted I take it as well, but none of them understood the connection I had with that diary. That diary had been my only best friend after Io had moved out; I resented and then denied accepting it. Later that evening, I saw Lilac using that dairy for herself, making collage spreads.

My heart shattered into countless pieces, my world crumbling around me as I witnessed the insensitive and ignorant behaviour of that annoying brat. It was a betrayal that cut me to the core. All I had hoped for was a gleam of empathy from Lilac, a semblance of gratitude akin to Io's, but instead, she was insufferable and unappreciative. Io was leagues above her. Yet, to this day, she fails to acknowledge her wrongdoings. And after all these years, unbelievably, she dares to claim that she discarded it because it looked like mere junk to her.

By then, I had lost my composure and had since begun yelling at her for the things that she had done to me. I could no longer pretend to be a sweet old sister.

I often hear my Mum telling me that I seem to hold onto grudges. It's something that I really dislike about myself as well. I wish I didn't feel so helpless, insecure and naïve at times. I know that lying in bed feeling miserable won't help, but it's hard to shake off these feelings.

Going to the university via local transport gives me some time to reflect on things, because these feelings don't usually affect me except when I am home.

University has been hard too. Mum feels that since I am not doing a medical degree, my life is supposed to be comfortable and uncomplicated, but they would never understand how I barely manage to stay on my feet and not pass out any second because college is hard, where everyone is in this strange, no-nonsensical roleplay. Students pretend to be really sweet. Teachers are all the same, "wannabe tough guys," trying to be all Miranda Priestly. Honestly, nobody is genuine there, which makes the place all the more exhausting and hostile. There are layers behind everything for no real reason.

RJ, Roderick Jagger, he is like the Father of assholes. He is just too intimidating to handle or even call out.

If I had a list of people I hated, he would be on top!

He has embarrassed me before everyone, time and again, and I don't want to be that person the class laughs at. This proposal was super important but I don't know what tomorrow will look like, now that Mum has talked to him.

It's high time now, and I should definitely nap off; I don't wanna drown myself in these thoughts again.!

I wake up to the noise of my sister running upstairs. I really don't wish to get into another fight with her, and I should just avoid talking to her as much as I can. I get up and slip into my casuals to go outside for a stroll with my headphones on; the only possible getaway there is now. She watches me go and does not attempt to stop me.

I come back home after about an hour and see my Father operating my laptop; I walk up to him since he is the only sane human I can talk to without fighting in the whole damn house.

Dad: "The system needed repairs, so I got the battery replaced. As for your project, keep your data elsewhere saved, too; big girl, things like this would keep on happening! You ought to be careful, you know. The guy barely managed to extract your files safely!"

This was literally the only good thing I had heard the entire day from Dad!

"And that's why I have got this for you!!" Lil'ass walked in and passed me a box with an ever-so-pathetic gaze on her face. I opened it and found a hard disk there. She bought it for me with her pocket money.

"I remember you asking for a hard disk a few days back! What's the next thing that you're gonna do? Keep it for yourself after I turn it down?"

The change in her expression was evident. I did not mean the words as they sounded, but the harm had been done.

Lilac: "Why do you always talk to me like that? I try to do everything to make you feel like an older sister and show that I care, but all you do is come and be this snobby person who just wants to prove that I am the worst. I said I am sorry; I know you worked hard for it, and I know that I have a bitter tongue, but that gives you no right to talk to me the way you do. I am careless, and I hate myself for that, but please stop!!! Stop treating me like trash!"

Her words were sincere. But my temper had moved beyond rationality.

"Yeah, just like you did with Io's Diary?" I smirk.

Lilac: "For crying out loud, it's been years now, why do we have to bring back that incident every damn time? Even then, I was as guilty of my mistake as I am today. All I try doing is to be in your good books, but you have been so distant from me. I try to make amends, but you always make me feel like a pest."

"Make amends by using it for yourself? Io was my only friend, and that diary was the only thing I ever possessed! You come up to show pity and then act like it never even mattered " I felt I was reaching my limits.

Lilac: "Your only possession? Do we not mean anything to you? During those years, I have tried to get closer to you so we could be like normal sisters, but you always push me away, like I mean nothing to you! And Io! Huh. Sure, your only friend! Your only friend who never contacted you after going, and so did you? Had she been so precious and dear, why didn't you? You just gave up on the treasured piece of "your soul?" Don't act so gullible! The world has made enough progress for you to find old and forgotten people. You are just a lonely and despairing person who loves to blame the circumstances for her own made-up misery. You love your design work, so why are you so afraid of your professors when you think you have done enough? And about that diary, that diary meant so much to you, and my diary was too uncool to even be accepted by you! I made a collage for you and wrote how I was so grateful to have you as my older sis, but for almost a week since that day, you refused to even look into my eyes! I was so shattered that I threw it away without you even looking at it once! What do you think? Only you have emotions? Give me a break!"

All this was too much for me to process. The world around me was at a standstill, or at least that's how it felt to me. I could only hear a loud, squawky sound in my ears after this. Lilac's lips were still moving. Despite fighting every day, I had never seen her so bitter and inflamed!

She was right, I could have contacted Io! Then why didn't I? Did I even mean to her what she meant to me, after all this time? I strangely found myself reflecting on whether my feelings of loneliness influenced my actions. My denial about the possibility that reaching out to her would not solve my problems or perhaps, even give any solutions, instead force me to confront the true causes of my emptiness.

It was a scary experience. As I saw my Mum running towards us, I began feeling lightheaded, and everything started to blur. The next thing I knew, I was on the ground. It was a frightening feeling that I never wanted to experience again...

The impact of her words was profound, causing me to black out. I didn't eat properly throughout the day, and then also went for a walk, further weakening my body.

I woke up to my mother's voice a few hours later. She had gotten food for me.

Mum: "That's why I ask you, girls, to adequately have all your meals and fluids regularly. I have had a word with your faculty, and they have said that they would only need the receipt for the replaced parts of the laptop, with the right date, and your work should be up to the mark."

"As for your sister, you guys should really talk; you both give each other a hard time, you know. She cried a lot when you fainted and made this food for you. She did not wish to face you, so she went to your aunt's place to stay the night. I think you both should talk things out and try removing all the loathing you've developed for each other over the years. Your expectations from each other have been so high ever since the start that you have forgotten that you are humans who tend to make mistakes. Accept the flaws, and you both will be better than ever!"

She is right, I always looked for Io in her and was disappointed every time, to the point that I had no hopes left!

I am the one at fault and I should try making amends, first thing tomorrow!

That reminds me, Io!

I pulled up my phone and opened my socials. 'What was her name!!!! Io..... Io.....'

'Iodice! What were her initials........'

'Elisa Iodice'

57 Elise Iodice? No way! But I don't even have another choice. I tried seeing all the profiles but could not find any! After hunting through all the profiles from all the social platforms, I still had no lead!

I tried searching for her brother, Enzo, and after going through a few profiles, I saw his face thumbnail in one of the IDs. It's an awkward hour, but let's try texting him to ask where these guys have been after all these years and if I could get in contact with Io. I text him;

Mauve: "Hey, it's me, Mauve, remember me from the neighbourhood street? How were you after all these years? And also, how is Io? Haven't heard from her ever since you guys moved to your new place, and Io stopped writing to me..."

I leave the phone, hoping to hear from him soon and get back to working on my project. I take my pills at three and crash off on the couch...

7th June 2015

I wake up and suddenly realise that Lil'ass is still not home. Whoa, that means an empty shower!!!

I get ready and head to the breakfast table 30 minutes before time. I packed my bag last night and made sure to not work on the table this time. For once, it feels so organised and peaceful. I glance over at Dad, who is watching some debate on the cable.

Man, it feels so weird when that Lil-ass is not home! I got ready so early! I sit back at the table to review my project again.

After half an hour of revising, I head towards the bus stop. I take the first bus, which drops me to the transit stop. The bus usually comes around 8:30 am and drops me off at college. I board the first bus and it's not even eight so there's hardly any crowd.

This way, I'll reach college an hour before, and I think out loud.

Lil'ass takes such a long time to take a shower.

What if it could always be this way? I think and laugh at the possibility! I open my laptop and proceed to work again.

CHAPTER 2
ABDUCTION

7th June, Continued…

I got off at the transit station and waited for the next bus. The bus took quite a while to arrive, but fortunately, I had some extra time today. When I boarded the bus, there were only ten other passengers: three lively 15-something-year-old girls, an elderly lady, and the ticket collector. I walked past them and took a seat in the second-to-last row. I plugged in my headphones to fully enjoy the suburban view.

Now that I have all the time to think (20 minutes, to be precise).

The Reason by Hoobastank it is.

"There are many things I wish I didn't do, but I continue learning…"

I shouldn't have said those things to her. Maybe we really need a fresh start. I'm not a perfect person; it's true. She deserved better. The best she did all this while was just to be herself. She could have played the imposter and tried to be Io, but she didn't. I was not the best sister either.

As I stepped onto the bus, the old lady got off while a few others boarded, including some girls from my college. Ugh, those girls are so annoying. I really wish I could adopt their carefree, impassive attitude and strut through life as they do.

At the next stop, a guy walked in and asked if he could take the seat beside me.

"Of course," I said, trying to act nonchalant.

It's not like I really care; the seat was empty anyway. Maybe I was better off not sharing my space with anyone.

Wait, did I say that too loudly? Darn, these headphones!

It's not that I'm not interested in boys. I find them attractive, but I don't think I am emotionally capable of engaging in a conversation without making myself look foolish.

Anyway, I look outside the window. We reach the outskirts of the city, and I see kids playing joyfully amongst themselves, their laughter resonating through the air, while towering trees reach up towards the endless sky, creating a breathtaking natural canopy. The views from where I stand are nothing short of amazing, filling me with a sense of peace and wonder.

But...

Wait. What place is this? This is not my usual route. Did I board the wrong bus?

I turn to look inside for the conductor, and.........
FU**KKKKK!!!

I see the conductor's face a few feet away from mine, shouting, "Surrender your phones, and any smart move will be your end!"

The bus has been hijacked. The driver calls him out! 'Souvik!!'

The conductor approached him and handed over a jute bag. He took away our phone and other belongings and put them in the bag near the door to keep them out of reach. While on the way, they stopped at a desolate place and threw all the phones into the sewage drain. Then, at intervals and varying distances, they discarded our belongings.

I am freaking out. Where am I? What did I just do? This is the wrong bus, oh my God!! What is happening?

I see all the people on the bus screaming for help! I stand there still with my hands behind my back! I see a girl taking out some of the hair accessories tied on her head to attack the conductor, but the driver sees her and shouts, "Souvik, look out, the girl behind you!!"

Souvik runs up to her and catches her head. His face turns red, and he snatches it off her head to throw it away. He then starts screaming like a madman, pulls out a gun and shoots her!

...

There is dead-drop silence. No one dares to move an ounce.

"We have dealt with fools like you before. You move, you die. You all are now the offerings to our God!" Souvik declares.

WHAT ON EARTH WAS THAT!??

Have I seen death with my naked eye? My heart starts pounding; my body is shivering with fear... but not as much that can catch the eye of the heartless man in front of me... Who are these people, and why are they even doing this!!! What is this? There's blood all over the place. And what God? What is this cult!? Is this a joke? A religious sacrifice? Political propaganda? What did we do? Why us? What is wrong with these people? I need to think of some way to flee.

He takes the girl's corpse to the front of the bus and wraps it up in rugs. They barely wipe the blood off the floor and throw out the body in the next sewage.

I have never seen such insanity in the name of sacrifice! The girl was protecting herself! Who are these monsters? I can't stay like this, but moving even an inch could be fatal; they can kill us all. I need to go home!!

He asks us all to sit and ties our hands to the seat in front. Then, he takes out a jar with pills and a bottle of some fluid. They look like sedatives.

"Take these like good boys or you die," he goes up to the guy in the first seat.

His eyes express desperate refusal, but he begs him to spare his life.

We have nothing to contact anyone around. How will we ever get out of here?

Souvik forcibly opens that guy's mouth and gives him the pill. He gasps into the ground, coughing and choking. Souvik then grabs his neck, pulls him close to pour the fluid inside his mouth, and jerks him back to his seat. The boy's body turns pale, and he coughs for some time, and then he faints.

"If you people don't want bad fortune upon yourself, then do as I saw, for as long as you follow me, you stay alive! The moment you don't, you just set an example for the rest!" He threatens.

He walks up to everyone seat by seat and passes on the pill. Nobody dares to revolt.

There are twelve girls and six boys alive on the bus. Our hearts were hammering our chests as we struggled against the restraints. Fear had consumed us.

He comes up to me, and I obediently take the pill with the fluid, avoiding any eye contact with him. I feel my body heating up almost instantly after taking it. My legs start to hurt, and I fall back to my seat. I felt a similar twisting of the stomach as last night; this is just worse. My forehead started sweating, and I could not hold back my tears. All my life flashes before my eyes, and my head starts to feel heavy...

All this pain continues for three minutes straight until I pass out.

CHAPTER 3
BLACK HOLE

I wake up and find myself in a huge dungeon! My hands and mouth are tied. I look back and see others from the bus as well. We all are sitting in one corner of the room.

This place is dark and eerie. Men are being beaten up and threatened to work like slaves. There are no windows in this place; it's cold and suffocating just to be in. I hardly see any light. There are tiny crevices that are barely letting any rays get in. The other corner of the room is stacked with animal skin and shreds of meat thrown in front. People are covered with rags.

What is this place? Why are people even existing here? This looks like a concentration camp. Is this where people are being offered to God?

I see Souvik and the bus driver walking up to check on us, holding a mug in their hands. Souvik goes around to each one of us and looks detestable. His eyes are red with lust and disgust. He gazes at us crookedly and grins to himself.

He approaches to walk up to me... I am shivering and am too afraid to even open my eyes. He politely asks me to open my eyes, but I resist and keep them shut.

I sense a loud blow as he grabs me by my hair and pulls it hard. I am strangling as he pulls my head in front of his face.

Souvik: "Who do we have here?"

"You don't have to be scared, lady. This is going to be your new home; don't be ashamed of anything around here! Everyone here will now be your family." (His tone suddenly amplifies)

"So shut this crap and look at me!!! Rojan, get the things here!"

(Points to the bus driver; he is another one of his subordinates)

Rojan comes back with a sack from the bus. He pulls out a knuckled ring and gives it to Souvik.

In a flash, he strikes my hair, chopping it off in seconds. My reflexes were too weak. My body couldn't respond to the speed at which it happened.

He holds my collar and tears my shirt off. I try to move, screaming, but my hands and mouth are painfully tied.

More of their men arrive and do the same with all the girls in the room.

Rojan holds me up against the ground and starts taking off all my clothes. He throws them all away, then takes out something from the sack and wraps me up in it.

Never have I felt so ashamed in my entire life. I'm crying, but nothing is coming of help now. My spirits are starting to give up. I scream and try biting him to escape. He throws me down the floor and smacks me till I quit!

I can feel the shiver down my spine on my naked body, with this sack they have used to cover us up. I could feel the motion of a bug running up my feet. I'm getting goosebumps, and my body starts to sense the sickness, and I'm having a twisting ache in my stomach.

I am desperately trying to make sense of all this... Why are they doing this to us... Is this what their God asked? This is pure insanity! Is this what the hell looks like? I have done bad things in my life, but I never felt that any of that was worth this!? Am I dead?

No, I can't be! I am feeling something that I have never felt before. The pain, the humiliation, the helplessness, the growling, the scar from his smack on my face, the shame of being naked in front of these people is FU*KING REAL!! But why are they doing this to us? Who are these terrorists holding us hostage?

After hours of this torture being done to all of us, a man comes up with a shackled chain and starts hooking us in a row, with Rojan untying us. They chain our legs through the long iron leg and proceed to blindfold us. They also stuff a dense ball of fabric in our mouths.

"Upfront!" Souvik commands and another man holds up as they take us on a haul. After walking for what seemed like ages, they knocked on a door.

"We have our bait here for you Master, anything else we can help you with?," Souvik declares but his voice is cracking.

"Get in," we hear someone from the other side.

"Oh Lord, here we have our atonement, six men and fourteen women from south of Desmsworth. We had to kill a misbehaving commuter, the driver, the conductor and his son. He saw us while we were taking the bus away. Yet, we have made sure to leave no eyewitnesses or digital footprints behind," Souvik insisted.

"Looks like you guys have done your work pretty smoothly without any suspicion, and you will be rewarded. You both have my word. We were running short on our deals, and we needed more mortals to keep up the supply. Malav and Raven have gone with their units and will be back soon with their stocks; this season looks very promising," said the man behind the table in a deep, calm voice. He did not sound older than in his 40s.

One girl screamed abruptly, and consecutively we heard a loud smack, and then she fell gasping to the ground, sobbing.

It was all so sudden and quick; we couldn't make out what was happening outside.

There was no sensation of anybody even moving. We could only hear the voices of these people...

All this is just manic psychosis. Everything about this place is cynical.

But did I hear things right? What is all this bullcrap!? Mortals? Stocks? Have we been trafficked? This can't be true, right? What are they going to do with us?

"DON'T WORRY MY PUPIL. CONSIDER ME AS YOUR PROTECTOR, YOUR CAREGIVER."

"We treat everyone here as our own. I will take care of you from now on, you will be given your food, clothing, and shelter and we will protect you from all the dangers of the world. All you need to do is obey me and you will remain alive!"

His men begin to take our blindfolds off.

He was a black-haired, well-groomed man in his late 30s; his clothes were polished, somehow giving an impression of an odd, misbegotten creature. He is extremely calm and secure, with an almost unnerving demeanour. His words were cleverly measured with a tone that was both sombre and intense. He seemed manipulative, methodical and deliberate in his own sinister ways...

A girl from the crowd starts howling with the fabric still stuffed in her mouth as the man touches her body.

"It's a pleasure to meet you, Avive. I am sorry if my men hurt you! Please be gentle with these ladies. Don't worry, I am nothing like them," the man comforts.

The girl hears this and is left in a standstill.

How did he know her name? We had been randomly picked from the bus by these madmen, but again how did he know her? The man takes the stuffed fabric out of her mouth.

"Who are you, and why did you bring me here? You monsters will be behind bars when I get out of this place!" she exclaims.

As she says this, we see her head freeze in mid-air as if it has been snatched from behind; nobody moved this whole time, and within moments, blood starts falling from her eyes as she collapses to the ground, weeping.

"Oh, that's so silly of me. I know everything about you all! I haven't introduced myself yet. I am Hadden. And from now on... you all are my responsibility. You all were destined to be here, and I am your protector, your God. You all ought to call me that only. Just know this thing about me; I can see it through you. I know you all too well, all your secrets, all that you had been trying really hard to hide from the world, just everything. You try to deceive me, and your traces will vaporise from the surface of Earth. I had been looking at you all for days... To let you mortals know more, your previous life has been obliviated. No one from there remembers you. You try escaping or contacting anyone, and they'll just shoo you away like a maniac."

"I AM YOUR DESTINY..."

"We all live happily like a family, with you all as my loyal associates, and I'll let you all live..."

Who is this man? There's something about him that's so serene yet fatale. His men were raging and dominating, throwing us around like vermin, but his demeanour is psychopathic.

This is no dream, nor am I in hell. Maybe he is right, and this is our destiny. So, he means to say we all are trapped, and we don't even try to escape?

What is this tomfoolery? Removing out names from the minds of people close to us? What is this? Some anti-hero fanfic? Why should we even trust anything he says!?

There's just so much that's hardly making any real sense. But I dare not say a word... I don't wanna end up like these other girls; there must be some way to escape. Till then, I must observe all things to play along. Can't threaten my life with mere futile rebellion. But what is the reality of this God of the madmen, and how are they still hidden from the world? I need to know what's behind this sect's motive and how he is so persuasive that these people are blindly following him. What has he done that these people consider him their God? He is calmly devious, but that's just not it.

For now, I must keep quiet for as long as I can and think of the right time to escape; I cannot give up on my family. I have to go back to Lilac and apologise for yesterday.

Hadden: "Boys, these guys must be hungry! Get them something to eat." They dash away as he commands. They came back with some fluid and food pills, they held us by the head and made us gulp a full bowl of the fluid. As soon as we consumed it, our bellies were surprisingly full. We lost our appetite.

In a swoop, the hues before my eyes began to change, and my life flashed before my eyes. I was laughing continuously. Lilac, Mum, Dad, Io… I could see their faces… I saw them running away from me…

Would I never see them again? Was Hadden not blabbering, and have we lost these people from our lives? My head started spinning, and I collapsed on the ground, trying to hold my body together, but my hands were no longer in my control. All I could remember was crying out streams of tears. The suffering was growing beyond endurance. But as I stopped, I could hear the rest of the people going through the same pain, too. My head hurts like hell. What have they fed us with? What's the worst they're gonna do to us?

After 10 minutes of agony and distress, everything felt blank….

Numb…

My body no longer feels like my own. It's as if my brain can no longer command my limbs. My mind is in isolation from my soma. As I'm trying to process what has happened to me, I begin to get up from the floor.

Wait what? I'm not doing this, but I can't stop myself. I look at Hadden, and he grins, looking at us. Is this… Telekinesis?

After some time, while we were having these internal battles with ourselves, I could overhear Hadden's voice from the other room.

Hadden: "You know our stocks have rotten. We need to ship them to the Rank D clients. They have the worst payment policies, and I do not intend to please them in any way. It'll be easy to shed off, so my new stock is ready for display. Everyone looks propitious. Malav and Raven would be back in an hour. We are going to have a grand season. The girls must be conscious by now; it's been more than five hours; go check for any major injuries or scars in their bodies and dispose of them with the prior stock if they do. Make your men conceal the scar; I don't want any hindrances with the payment on each one. Verify the terms and no negotiations; I trust you; do not disappoint me, Rojan."

Sell them? Things are getting just too complicated for me to understand.

We all automatically start marching forward... I look at my feet, trying to gain control, but I just can't stop them! And it's just not me. The rest of the people also march ahead to a side and sit; I see another bunch of 50-something people as they walk in. They must be the older ones Hadden was talking about. Both men and women had their bodies heavily bruised.

The hopelessness in their eyes was way beyond ours. The craving for a life was non-existent. There was contentment in their eyes with the place. They wouldn't make a move on their own from the fear of being noticed, as they stood in a perfect parade, equidistant from each other.

After they all positioned themselves, Rojan walked in.

"EXAMINE!" Hadden exclaimed.

At once, all the men stood in front of one another and stripped themselves away. Their bodies were full of bruises and injuries. My eyes weighed heavy at the sight of this terror. No one attempted to resist like it was a daily chore. His men went around every man of the parade, scrutinising them for major deformities and further segregating them into groups based on the severity of the scars.

Group 1: Had minor cuts here and there.

Group 2: Had deeper wounds and clot marks.

Group 3: People with permanent body damage, internal dislocation, etc.

Hadden: "Asher, take Group 2 to the Mediterranean belt and extract all the functioning organs from people Group 3; the rest of their flesh could be used as a feedstock."

This is pure insanity!!! Why isn't anyone doing anything about this!? What in the world have we ever done to them to deserve any of this!?? Why doesn't anyone know about this filthy business!! Are they killing people for diseases that can be medically operated upon?

The men gathered to follow as instructed, tears gliding through the eyes of the people who were now going to be slaughtered in the name of their 'fate,' with no attempts at revolting. The rest of us got up from there and walked towards a huge hall. Close to fifty of us girls then cushioned and slept on top of one another.

CHAPTER 4
TRADE SECRETS

At dusk, we get up again, unconsciously and start moving out, handcuffed with our legs still chained to each other. We arrive at a hall with a high ceiling, this place feels like a world in itself. The space was so dreadfully gigantic and isolated that we could barely see beyond a few feet.

This looks like a prison cell! One of his men comes up and releases our cuffs, leaving our feet in shackles. An electric sensation ran abruptly in our heads, and we started moving towards the rooms.

I move towards a room that reads '1022-Mauve- 20.' 1022, my prison cell number. All these things further induced me to postulate what Hadden said was sincere. That, maybe, we were destined to be here, and he had a close eye on us all along? They knew my name and age before I even knew of this place's existence.

Besides my room, I see three girls standing, which read '1019-Avive- 23,' "1020-Akia-21," and '1021-Astra-16.' The girls standing before me appeared related with similar facial build, seemingly siblings, or maybe that was just presumptuous of me. We hear a loud thump and enter our rooms in unison. For them, we were just toys being played with.

The room has this empty space with bare bedding with a stack of quilts, a window that can barely let any sunshine in, a broken ceiling fan, some pieces of chalk, a mantle with a few obscurely-fashioned clothing shreds and some manuscripts; the room is connected to an unaccustomed lavatory, leaky with a recurring dripping sound.

There were no doors in the rooms, it was as if they were confident that we wouldn't even attempt any escape, or they probably knew we couldn't since Hadden had an eye on us anyway. We could see everything, there was this uncomfortable transparency where everyone's privacy was non-consensually shared with everyone else. But even then, no one dared to near the doorway. Electric cables were lying all over the place.

I went inside to use the lavatory but felt like puking at the very glimpse of it. It was a pathetic sight. I moved to the other side to take the bucket to pour water around to clean it but the water flow was as sparse as the living conditions of the place. I couldn't hold my bladder anymore and I desperately needed to pee. I ran looking around the place for something else to clean the dump hole.

Ultimately, after fifteen minutes of struggle, I took the old scraps of paper and closed all of my senses to use that shithole, trying extremely hard not to puke.

It had already been the worst day of my life...

I came out near the bed stack and crashed myself to sob my heart out. They had been mistreating us from the moment we set foot in this place. This had been the only moment since our abduction I had been alone away from the insanity spread by that psychopath Hadden.

I cried all night till my eyes blurted out. For the first time, I felt free to express myself after all the molesting harassment, slapping and hair-snatching. It's almost inhumane how Souvik grabbed me as he chopped my hair off., and Rojan stripped me off...

I turned to see my upper limb bruised with marks of his fingers wrapping around my arm.

***

I was asleep when I heard something amidst the dead silence of the night; it must be around eleven in the night. I hear slow steps and heavy breaths of someone hovering from a distance. The horrors of someone coming here pushed me to the back of the bed as I squeezed myself into the tiniest forms I could. I hear the steps approaching my room...

And then leaving, a trail of bafflement followed...

I stayed there, trying to figure out who it was, but it was too dark to make out.

I wondered, the sound of the steps was rather soft, unlike Rojan's or Souvik's. Someone must inspect the area all night to keep an eye on everyone. Nobody can escape this trap so easily. And no one would be so brainless to get themselves killed, too.

I waited there for some time to see anything in the depths of the darkness, but nothing happened, and I unconsciously fell senseless into deep sleep.

My senses revoke when I heard strange blisters of distant bawling as if someone was being beaten up, as did the dripping sound of the leaky washroom tap. I knew I couldn't do anything, so I immersed myself back into the insentient realm and shut all my hearing senses.

The next morning, there was a sudden chaos as his men rushed inside each room. Rojan forced himself onto my room and gushed the food pills and the fluid in my mouth while I was still unconscious.

It was now that I adored the way Mum would wake me up in the morning. I'm guessing this is probably how they are going to wake us up every day.

He ordered us to reach the main hall in thirty minutes.

I picked up the rags kept there for us. An oddly fashioned rag in khaki, loosely woven pullover hand-stitched, barely held together, with two openings on the sides to slide our arms in. There were some scraps of beige fabric kept there. I decided to wrap them around my hips and chest as undergarments and then put on the pullover rag.

I knew for a fact that this place had nothing better to offer than this, so after episodes of panic, I made the best of the available resources.

After a little while, there was a loud bang of a horn, and we began marching our way out of the room to the main hall.

It was a real astonishment to see that none of the rooms in the entire place had doors. Was Hadden so secure about himself and his powers? They did not even really try to imprison anyone, as if he knew that no one could run. Given that no one remembers us in the outside world, no one has ever tried escaping from here either! It haunts me to even think that I would be face to face with Mum, Dad and Lilac, and they wouldn't recognise me. The very thought gave me goosebumps.

This can also all be a hoax; I won't believe in anything that he tells me to believe. I need to get out of this place... There must be something more than what they say, and I need to find that loophole to escape.

As we stand there in a queue, I see a girl standing right next to me. There was something odd and disturbing about her. I recognise her from yesterday, Avive, if I'm not wrong. Her eyes were swollen, and her posture was bent and weak; she looked physically very tired, and there were clot marks on her arms and neck as if someone grabbed her fragile neck with force. Initially, I thought she would be an insomniac like me, but by every other thing that I observed about her, my speculations about her seemed to change.

We moved through the hallway to the main dungeon, a lot of people were standing there in two perfectly spaced rows, blindfolded. These must be the batch of people Hadden was talking about yesterday, brought in by Malav and Raven.

All of them look miserable and hopeless. They have no idea of the hell they have entered. We cross through that room into another passage leading to a hall!

The place is filled with hanging parts of flesh and meat, unrecognisable as being of a man or beast. It was a huge space with close to twenty large tables, with an organised section for different segments and two subsections at the end of each for what looked like assembling. Starting with collecting, cutting, cleaning, fur removal, washing, and packaging. I see several other men coming in with deadstock of hounds and cervids on the trail cages, who had been shot. Walking past him was another man who carried stocks of sirenians. This was a slaughterhouse, engaging in illegal slave trade and animal poaching!

There were the other older men from yesterday. They were all practically practising gun-firing to work with Raven and Malav; I guess this is what they traded for their lives. Being the subordinates of the very people who did bad to you and then doing the same with other innocent people and animals.

The set-up worked like a small-scale organised cottage industry, except everyone acted like they had no mind of their own. Everyone was assigned an activity, which they had to perform with precision.

The deadstock would arrive and would be sent to a huge bath, that can hold a quintal of stock, they'll be washed there with a high-pressure water. Then the stock would be divided amongst the twenty tables spread across the hall. Each table was 30 feet long and at most three people were allotted the same activity on a table.

The stock, depending on the end use, would be distributed across the tables, which covered:

1. consumption
2. cosmetic purpose
3. upholstery
4. clothing
5. pharmaceuticals

After coming from the bath post-cleaning, it would be sent to different departments, where they would be cut according to the industry it is being packed for, sanitised to cover up the gunshot clot marks and properly labelled and packed in designated boxes. There would be special stocks placed for specialised organs/units, such as kidney, bone marrow or liver when they were extracted in perfect working conditions. All the boxes would further be passed through a scanning machine for quality assurance.

THIS WAS JUST, PURE INSANITY...!!!

This needs to freaking stop! I wanted to puke right then and there, but I hardly had any food in my belly to be flush out! Apart from the strict regulations being followed in the entire process, these cannibals dared to corrupt the stocks with the flesh of humans they would slaughter as part of their clearance of the older stock.

Through this chain, they branched out the chemistry that made the food pills for us, the one they had been feeding us with. Which was high in carbs and protein, to avoid maintenance and feedstock wastage.

* * *

We begin to move to our designated workstations; God forbid I'm in the packaging section, which does not involve physically touching bare flesh as much. As Hadden has us all wired, we are doing the jobs as experts in the profession despite never having seen anything like this before. I kept my eyes shut throughout the process as I could not bear the horrors of even peeking at what we were really doing.

As I open my eyes to peep, the girls around me are also visibly horrified and disgusted by their own actions. The atmosphere grows more suspicious and eerie with each passing second, casting a shadow of fear over the entire place.

This went on till daybreak when we all just sprang away from the tables and went close to one side of the walls. Around thirty of us arrived there and sat down fairly close to each other as we lay down on the ground. We all were in such near proximity that it was one person over the other! This girl 'Giavanna' had her legs over my stomach. A strange sensation ran over us as we forcibly shut our eyelids in a symphony as a sign for us to sleep.

Hadden even had control over parts of our bodies.

After about an hour, we all harmoniously wake up and get back on the same tables to work. Working there and listening to the conversations of his men, I managed to deduce a lot of things about their functioning.

Turns out the people who transport these stocks to the clients are the ones who worked here once. They must have been really old and trustworthy. And Hadden gets the least from the work he does. Rather, he is gathering more and more organisations to become any part of their supply chain and help him expand the trade!

But what would he get out of this? Brutally killing animals for their meat, enslaving humans, and controlling whatever they do. I am sure this human is way more insane than this! Is he doing all this to officially declare himself God!?

Although, I really think he does not know a real thing about God! His concept of being godly is completely twisted and I would wanna know how he is doing it. Gathering all these people, making this cult of which nobody wants to be a part!

I see this 16-year-old beside me; she has a straight face, and she is at her age of being carefree and enjoying life. What is she doing?! I see her heavy eyes, crying for help, and a teardrop falling every once in a while. She wants to go to her mother, her past life! We all do! We don't know for how long are we going to be trapped here?!!!

The clock strikes 5, and we leave our tables and go to one corner, wash all our hands and go back to stand in a line. Malav and Rojan come with several others with the food pill and water. This time, they graciously ask us to take them, and since we are being controlled anyway, we take him without rebellion. They did not tie us into those things again. I would love to burst their bubble of trust one day. Their faith in Hadden is fearfully superstitious.

We go back to our cell; there's finally some water coming. I clean up the mess I made in the morning. Take a shower, wash my clothes and get into a newer pair. The day had been shockingly tiring. I could not take it anymore, as I crashed onto the bed that very instant and fell asleep...

CHAPTER 5
LILAC

Nightmare

After a tiring day, I was fast asleep when on the sudden spur of a moment, I heard a booming thump on the floor, I sprung from the bed. I was so alarmed that I ran to see who was there at the front door, no other had turned up there till then. Upon pushing the front door open, Lilac entered.

I went berserk!!

Why has she come here? This place is extremely dangerous for her to even think of coming...

Mauve: Lilac, why in hell are you here?

Lilac: Don't worry now, I've come here to rescue you. Mum and Dad haven't stopped crying since the day you left. We have visited almost every police station in the area to file your missing complaint. But now, I'm here and won't leave without you...

Mauve: All that is fine, baby sis. But you need to run away from here. These guys are extremely gruesome and dangerous. They'll trap you, too, if they see you here.

Lilac: I told you I'm not leaving without you.

Mauve: Lilac, this is not the time to act stubborn! Leave from here at once!

> [She didn't understand how grieved the situation was, and I would lose my temper. Her determination to take me back weakened, and a tear flowed down her cheeks.]

Lilac: You never understand. You are doing this to us deliberately.

> [How could I even explain to her that I was saving her from him? He could never know of her... I couldn't hold back as I started crying too and continued begging her to leave.]

Mauve: Just tell me how did you come here... I'll follow you back, I promise. Listen to me now, and I will be with you guys very soon...

"What is going on here?"

I turned around to see Hadden standing there...

My heart suddenly pounded against my chest, my pulse racing. With a sudden feeling of suffocation, I struggled to catch my breath. The icy sensation in my feet made it difficult to find my balance as I leapt out of bed, consumed by disorientation.

It was all a bad dream.

This was just a bad dream...

Thank God...

I took a deep breath...

It was 3:30am, and everything around was at a standstill. I looked around and it was just... dark... I took my moment to absorb what I had been through in my dream...

Lilac must never be here!

My determination to leave the place grew as she might never come here to find me... and that mustn't happen, EVER!

I couldn't imagine my life without her... She had been with me for so long, no matter how annoying, but I just could not imagine without her being around.

The Birth of Lilac

I still remember it so vividly...

I was 6 years old, and we were in the process of getting Mum hospitalised. I had never seen my Mum this helpless and screaming so painfully. We were all running around chaotically, trying to find someone who could attend us. Her panic grew tenfold every time she looked at my face. I could sense the heat of the situation, but with every passing second, my faith was weakening as the pace of Dad's footsteps increased.

For as long as the light of the Emergency Room was lit, we could feel my mother's body as well as our hearts fighting battles. The hostile smell of uncertainty hung heavy in the air, mingling with the distant sounds of beeping monitors and hushing voices. In that stark, fluorescent glow, we could feel my mother's body battling against the unknown, her every breath a testament to resilience. Our hearts mirrored the struggle; each beat was a prayer for her recovery, a plea for strength. Time seemed to stretch endlessly in that space, fighting a hopeful war within us.

I overheard Dad talking to his brother about sending me to Dayville Junior Secondary School and making a will to pass me the wealth that he had accumulated along with my Mum's savings. For extremely strong reasons, he had made up his mind not to live in a world without Mum, even if it meant leaving me behind alone. It was then that I was beginning to comprehend his tormenting line of thought, with such little understanding of the world. That day, the doctor stayed in the operating theatre the whole night without giving us any verdict, which further amplified our anxiety.

Dad forced me to send off to my aunt's place at night, and I would go around attacking anybody who even moved to get near me. That day, he got so agitated by my stubbornness that he held me by the collar and slapped the soul inside of me. I could see his eyes burning red with a helpless rage as my skin froze numb. I left the place at once and did not visit the hospital the next day. He called my aunt to check up on me, but I refused to speak to him. I would cry all night at the belief of not being around my parents and all the miseries I was being put through with nobody talking to me about what I wanted, questioning the very existence of Divinity and the Universe that dared to take my caregivers away from me. Being trapped in the very conflict of being left alone gave chills to my gut, severely affecting my health.

The following day, I went to the hospital to pay my Mum a visit. My Father was nowhere to be found in the entire block. I tried to find my aunt, whom I then saw at the other end of the hallway, running towards me with heavy tears in her eyes...

"Go visit your mother in that room," she yelled, pointing at a distant room. I rushed there and saw my mother lying on the bed, pale and weak, with my Father crying on the lower side of the bed. Dad rose from the bed as I entered and ran towards me to lift me up in his arms and said, 'The surgery was a success, Mauve. You are now an elder sister!'

The world around me froze again, but this time with initial numbness and then delight!

I am an elder sister. What does that even mean?

I AM AN ELDER SISTER???

I could see my Dad's eyes gleaming with tears of joy after all these terrible days of grief and uncertainty. A few hours later, my Mum gained back consciousness and cried as she saw me... She hugged me tight and apologized for making us go through all this. For good reasons, I knew that she should have never done that.

As for my baby sister, she was born as the little hope of our family, the reason we smiled after days of misery. I swore that day that whatever comes to her goes through me.

I never really thought that I could ever be happier!

Holding her for the first time in my arms, I was sure that I would name her 'Lavender' or ' Lilac,' so she was as similar to me as could be! We both would literally be the shades of royalty, humility and passion.

It's still vivid in my memory. On the 17th of September, our Princess came to our lives to make it better and to teach us that even on the darkest of days, you can find your sunshine. She was the sole reason why our family was whole. Thinking back now, it kind of feels too innocent of me as I never made out 'why Mum was gaining all that weight.' She had been pregnant all along, but her case had some major complications during the stages of delivery.

'No matter how insanely sick I behave around her, there hasn't been a moment that I have cared any less about her, maybe over the years. I have let hatred and ignorance get the better of me. That was the first instance of me being aware of the dark thoughts about death. The most I can do now is stay alive and get away from here and hope that she remembers me when I get back there...

I sob at the thought and fall asleep.

I hear a distant sound after a while; it must be one of his men... My throat is running dry of thirst; I need water... I head towards the water jar kept on the bedside, but it's empty... I cannot wait till the morning to get it! I sense someone approaching my room, but I cannot see who it is in the dark. I shout, "Please give me some water!!!" He does not respond. I keep screaming, but the footsteps eventually fade away...

I don't understand; who is this walking alone in the depths of the night, not even helping or responding to anyone! I have to find out who it is and how they manage to get out of their room...

I swallow up my saliva and attempt to push myself back to sleep. All I hear is the chanting of a hesitant fan, whispering the noise of its own dysfunctional melancholy; the hounds howled at the top of their lungs, mourning those who were massacred by the beasts who call themselves 'Messengers of God.'

Weirdly enough, this howling reminds me more of my home and childhood.

I had my fears of one day facing the devil under my bed, I see the devil now... I see him with my eyes wide open...

As a kid, I was afraid of the dark because I always thought that the darkness would consume me... But now, it's this darkness that reminds me we are all under the same stars. and maybe there is no such thing as 'Fate' or 'The End,' merely the acceptance of it!

There might not be a tomorrow again! But I guess it was Lilac. It had always been her, and she was all we could think of! She saved us...

She saved us from this hollow nothingness because she reminded me that once tomorrow comes, she'll be right beside me.

* * *

"Wake up, you grumpy pigs!!!"

And here we go again...

I get out of bed, drink plenty of water before doing anything, and then calmly take my food pills without any signs of rebellion.

The day commences as usual, starting with barely dripping water in the tap, so I turn to use the papers. As I continue to do it, I get a weird feeling that one day, I might get used to all of it. I do my laundry and wear the ones I washed yesterday. Being alive here now is only possible if *I do as Romans do...*

We come out of the rooms as we hear the morning bell. At this point, they do not even attempt to chain us up. Their faith in us is almost haunting. We hear another thud and form a line. I see girls with faces unfamiliar to me from yesterday. I wish there was a way for me to communicate with my fellow prisoners.

As we march out, I do my best to scan all corners of the place, creating a mental picture without moving too much to avoid suspicion.

We reach back to the main "Room of Slaughter " with two new groups brought in today by the squads of Malav and Raven. I wonder what filthy tasks they will be assigned to do. Before we start our work for the day, Hadden walks in to greet all of us with a warm smile.

Hadden: "Hello, everyone. I apologize for not being able to meet with you all yesterday, as I was busy welcoming a new group. I am glad to see that you are all starting to adjust to this place and that your bodies are also adapting to the demands of this environment. Unfortunately, the packages we sent yesterday were not in great shape, and I received complaints from the client about the quality. Since it was your first day, I decided not to take any action against you. I will give you a week to improve, and I hope you will learn quickly. However, if we continue to compromise on our promises, there will be consequences. Batches 2 and 3 will be assigned to manage work in sectors B and C immediately, as we currently have enough workforce here. You are all dismissed. Thank you."

He leaves as he says this.

What does he mean by 'not good shape?' I am sure none of us would be killing living beings and perfectly slicing the pieces in our backyards... Don't really know how long we have to play along with his act!

As I approach my table, I see the siblings alongside me again. Akia and Astra? I see tears in the eyes of the youngest one, Astra, she mustn't be older than 16... No wonder this would have been just way too much for her to handle.

As we stand waiting for the stock to be cleared and brought to our tables, I see that girl in Avive's arms again. There are some deep blue blotches around her wrist. These weren't there the last time I saw her! It looks as if someone held her arms forcibly to drag her. Souvik and Rojan were on the bus when we came here, but I remember them not getting as close to touching her. This must be from her past life, I think, and proceed to work again...

CHAPTER 6
FETISH

New Bonds

After another exhausting day, we return to our cells. Our bodies are gradually adjusting to the torment, leaving me feeling less repulsed and more despondent.

It's like being adrift in the ocean, with only thoughts of reaching the shore and the distant horizon as the sole motivation.

I sit, leaning against the wall, as I scribble on the floor, thinking about school and my family and how thankless I was to them in every moment I spent with them!

Maybe I chose to be that way because I was tired! Tired of failing to meet people's expectations of me and vice versa. From being people-pleasing to a baddie, all of this was my defence mechanism. Defence of not giving any tangible hope to anyone who deemed themselves worthy of having expectations from...

I would randomly beat up anyone who ever tried to tease Io. Kinda loved doing it too. But then, accepting the reality of living a life without her was a lot for me to digest.

I felt like I had nobody, and every other person would leave me the same way…

Playing these human games in the endless mental fight for attention seemed amusing to me. I have been an introvert for as long as I can remember. However, that doesn't mean I never sought validation from the people around me.

'I have been an introvert too, all my life!'

I heard someone speak from the other side.

Am I hearing voices? I thought to myself.

'No stupid, you are just thinking out loud!'

The voice said cheerfully. I turned cherry red with embarrassment.

"By the way, my name is Avive. It was getting too gloomy out here. I've been alone for 2 days now, so I thought, why not just talk to someone around?" She was an extremely warm character, and I liked how she was so approachable.

'Hi Avive, my name is Mauve. I saw you around. Aren't you supposed to be one of the siblings?'

Avive: 'Siblings? I don't have any siblings. That's Akia and Astra. They have been around me since I was a kid. We were going to the university together when Souvik abducted us.'

'Ya, right. Since you all would always be around, I thought you were... But that was pretty bold of you. What did you do out there to The Lord on the first day?'

Avive: 'Who, Lord? That Hadden guy?'

'Please lower your voice. If they overhear us, we'll be in serious trouble!'

Avive: 'Aren't we in a lot of trouble, anyway? Then why be such a scaredy cat, my girl?'

'I'm not scared, just cautious. I don't want to get into any trouble and waste my life out here before escaping...'

Avive: 'You Plan on Escaping!!!'

[As she rose she said this, I could deduce by the frequency and distance of her voice]

'Keep it down!!!! Avive. You will get the both of us killed!'

Avive(chuckling): 'Don't worry, the worst they can do is just smash our faces against the wall or kick us to the ground!'

'Are you extremely bold, straight-up stupid, or plainly indifferent? It's hard to make out!'

Avive laughed.

Avive: 'You're really sweet, Mauve. I love your name! But ultimately, it's just gonna be one hell to another. I don't think there's any escape for me. I don't want to go back to my past life... So, technically, I have no place to go...'

She seemed more mature for her age; with every word she said, there was another hidden wound. Her will to live had now touched the zone where it was nothing more than a joke! I dared not ask her anything further, but it was nice to know that I had someone around whom I could talk to!

The next day, we went to work again in the main hall. Avive and I had the same task of covering the packaging again. She smiled at me with a broken nose; I chuckled cheerfully as I looked at her!

She introduced me to others, Akia and Astra, who were her childhood friends. Giavanna, Prisca and Sunashi became their friends in the dungeon. It was almost hilarious to see how we all were in-mates in misery! We worked through the day, passing glances at each other as we were all prohibited from speaking while working. But after work, we pretended to finish off the pending tasks when all the others had left!

Sunashi was a 26-year-old. She was completing her PhD in Micro-biological Sciences, at the university. She lived Downtown and had to commute every day for work. She had a high-headed and upright persona. Despite being terrorised by the happenings of the dungeon, she was the one most firm and the strongest when it came to holding back her tears.

Prisca and Akia were in their early twenties, high-spirited, and carefree. Both of them were sophomores like me, studying in the departments of Space Communication and Visual Design, respectively. Prisca cherished her previous life and was eager to leave this place. I found her as my partner in crime. Akia was Avive's close friend and Astra's sister, which meant that we were definitely going to get along well this time!

Giavanna and Astra became friends in the dungeon after realising that they had met at their 12th-grade's Farewell Eve. It turned out that they had also seen Lilac at the same event. It was a small world, indeed! I was glad to have found these people because they made my stay in the dungeon a little less terrifying. It was comforting to have found friends in such a miserable situation!

I returned back to my room, had another light-hearted conversation with Avive and for the first time, went to sleep a little less terribly...

Mistress of the Night

... I was fast asleep when a certain wave of thunder ran along my spine; I was so tired after the whole day's chaos that I only wished to escape...

Suddenly, my eyes opened wide, and I stood up and started walking.

It was Hadden, I was sure...

but I couldn't understand how to stop this; I came out from my cell and walked through the corridor. The sound of the other girls banging their floors in an attempt to stop me could be understood clearly. I understood that it wasn't just one person who was sleepwalking at night. But probably a different girl every night... I could feel my whole body shaking as to why he would summon me so late, trying my best to contain my breath...

I enter his room, which is a huge-walled room with dim lighting.

The feeling was unreal...

This was the first time I was near the devil himself... There was a choking sensation in my throat as my body failed to take in the oxygen with my rigorous breathing. He had wine in his hand, and he began pouring it slowly into the glass. I was shivering painfully as a drop of sweat dripped down my face, and my toes ran cold as I stood there, waiting impatiently... My body behaved so strangely that I could simply not comprehend how to process everything happening around me.

He took the glass, walked towards the couch on the other side of the room, and positioned himself comfortably. As he sat down and took a sip of wine, another thunder ran through me, and my feet started walking towards him. The horrors of my head were coming true, and all I could do was beg God to stop me from all this. My face turned red out of helplessness, and my cries for help accelerated with each step that I took towards him...

Upon approaching him, my hands began taking pieces of clothing off my body, and I sat next to him. I just had a fabric around my abdomen.

He was doing this... for himself...

He was literally using his psychic powers to give himself this pleasure. I was stunned by his ability to even think of something as awful as this. My hands moved towards him as I unbuttoned his pants and pulled them off his legs, gradually moving on to his briefs and removing them, too, revealing his genitalia.

I felt despairingly helpless, and by now, my burning red eyes swarmed a teardrop down my face, denser than ever... I felt like slapping myself and banging my head against the wall for even daring to do such a horrendous act. He took his hand and held my face, then waved his fingers across my cheeks, behind the ears, towards my neck. My body was shivering with loathing. My hatred for him skyrocketed every second.

He had a calm, almost satanic gaze on the facade. I stood up and turned around as he took a careful analysis of me and my body, wavering his finger all over the breaths of my body. He forcibly snatched off the fabric piece that had covered my lower abdomen, stripping me naked.

"Today, you get to be my 'Mistress of the Night!' " he screamed, proclaiming himself as the only higher power with devilish pride.

I held and pushed him towards the centre of the room, on the bed, opening my hair as I pulled out his vest. There was an awful terror in my scarlet stares of torture and disbelief. I was on the bed, naked, crying endlessly, listening to all his lies... He came towards me and made me sit on the bed, shoving another pill followed by some tonic in my mouth. My eyes were bleeding tears, and my body was soaring with pain... He pulled my face closer and kissed me passionately with his eyes closed.

Another shiver ran through my body, and I leaned toward him and placed my body above his, my hands wavering and moving towards his lower abdomen, slowly reaching his groin, then slowly started giving him the job he desired.

With every passing second, I felt a piercing pain of constant stabbing onto my soul... The life inside of me was dying as each teardrop rolled down my cheeks onto the sheets. I tried to scream at the top of my voice, but every time I tried, he would shove his genitals into my face... This went on endlessly till he reached the paramount of his pleasure... and after two hours of harvesting his telekinetic desires, he climaxed by splashing more odium for himself onto my face...

He pulled the sheets out and tried to wipe away this newfound hatred from my body. My eyes were struck at the door as the only means of the short-term escape conception. I did not know what more to expect of this place, as by each passing day, I would hate my fate even more... He stood up from the bed to clean himself and returned after fifteen minutes of taking a shower. He took a pill from the table that was placed beside the bed and forced it onto my mouth, just like the last time.

He lay on the bed beside me, waving his hand over my face, and began speaking for the first time in the whole night, "You know Mauve, I really love your name. And trust me, you are the most unique one from the whole lot! I had my eyes on you since the day you came. I am going to be completely honest with you : I don't do this for pleasure. Otherwise, I'd be running around jerking off to all the girls here. I do all this just to not feel lonely ..."

[This time, the sedatives he gave would make us forget about everything that happened to us as his Mistress]

I was hardly interested in comprehending what he had just said and could feel my body sink, and soon, I was dozing off into a painful line of thought. I never thought I hated men the way I did. Hadden reminded me of the very first incident that made me hate men so much...

The Story of Rian

I was a freshman in college when I first encountered such a dismissal of my fortune. All that had ever happened to me up till that moment seemed to be flowers and roses... I desperately wanted to move out from home for once in the name of higher education, but my parents' fights increased each and every day. They ensured that Lilac remained unaware of all this. Yet, I fully understood that they were deeply committed to each other and could not bear the thought of being apart despite having occasional, uncomfortably painful arguments.

I had made up my mind to leave the city entirely to start a new life, but it was after Mum's absolute reluctance and the clash of our huge-headed egos that I could not. I barely spoke to anyone at home for close to a month; I would stay outdoors through the day and then return late at night, entering my room directly from the back terrace pathway. My Mum was immune to this behaviour, so she would keep food for me in my room.

It was during this time that I met him...

We had to prepare for the university's fest to be held within two months of my being in college. I was sure that classes wouldn't keep me occupied enough and at that time I was willing to do anything that could potentially fulfill my desires to not be home and also, to jump scare my inner social angst.

As a part of the Event Management Team, we were assigned the task of putting up all the banners and flyers on the entire campus, and we had to do all this literally within just 5 days, starting from coordinating with the graphics team and the printing vendor, ensuring the quality of the print to perfectly put it up, with the Crew. All of this was totally new for me, and I was pretty excited about it, too, in the added hopes of making a lot of friends, maybe someone like Io as well! One of whom I felt was Rian.

He was the usual, dark and handsome, lean and 6-feet-something guy; he did not have any specific physical attribute that was attractive enough to make any girl fall head over heels for him... The only way he was even barely detectable from that crowd was because he was a sophomore, and most of us were freshers.

We spent the first two days arranging for the posters, which wasn't easy at all since these vendors are no less than dementors who missed no chance of sucking the life out of us. The pressure of finishing the task was extremely high, and that's when I worked pretty closely with him. He surely did not seem like someone I would be instantly infatuated with, but upon working together, we hit the suitable cords, and I kind of grew on him! We finished off the task quite at the brim of the situation, and the event ended pretty well. I was with him and his friends throughout the fest and had an absolutely amazing time. We were amidst the closing, which was the concert by 'ZEN!!!;' I had been literally obsessed with him since I was 15, and I knew all his songs word by word!

Everyone was overjoyed with all the screaming as the showdown song encored; they started showering fireworks up the sky and blew purple hearts up in the air. The gleams were high, and the energies of the entire concert peaked; all of us were beaming across when Rian held me by the arm and lifted me up in the open. I got freaked out for a second, but looking at him doing this, I paid no heed cause I could trust him with this! He put me back on the ground, smiling and hugged me tight; I could feel the butterflies fluttering and dancing with exuberance. After what felt like an eternity of compassion, he gave a peck on my lips. My heart skipped a beat as my world was at a standstill...

All this time, I hated even the thought of being around my family since all the drama began, and I was really hoping for it to get away. But after months of playing the victim of my circumstance, I found a reason to feel alive instead of avoiding every aspect of my reality.

My cheeks were flushing red as I went back home. Mum saw me sneaking in and just smiled, looking at my face. I was too easy to be caught, and being a rightful adult, I wasn't in any mood to conceal anything either! I went to bed with butterflies in my stomach, but I hit a certain low, realising he was going to leave for a week to the country.

Everything started seeming dreamy ever-so-suddenly... I also began interacting with my family as I was mostly in light air. All I cared about back then was to meet him again.

After what felt like another eternity of sorts, he came to the university. I finished my classes and went to meet him. He had called me to the 7th floor of the building, where he would have his classes. I entered his classroom as everybody had left. He gave me a headband; I looked at it and laughed cheerfully. It was too sweet of him to give me that! I had gotten gifts before, but this had been the only one that gave me butterflies. We chatted for a while and then planned to watch a movie together over the weekend.

We went to the theatre and had a great time dissecting every scene and making fun of all the characters. I had informed my Mum that I'd be coming home late. The movie ended somewhere around 11 pm, and as we were walking back home, he pulled me to the side of the road, held my face with his palm and tried kissing me ferociously. As he was doing that, his other hand grabbed me by my hips and pulled it closer to his body. His fingers entered beneath my jeans.

I was caught off-guard and got extremely furious by all this. I pushed him away like a fierce lioness and, within a breath, ran away from there...

There was a point where I did not understand the roads anymore but still did not dare to turn around. I found myself lost in the middle of the road and had no idea which way to go. I stopped to ask a man, who looked at me with disgust. I couldn't understand! Why would someone react so viciously to someone pleading for help? I looked out the window of a nearby car and saw my face smudged with lipstick. I sat down on the pathway and screamed out aloud, crying.

It had been after years that I put my trust in someone, but he ended up being like this. I knew there would be more than just this behind it. I wiped off my face and marched my way back home. I reached home around 2:15 am, and my Mum was heating up with anger; I did not want to face her. I had no energy to argue with her or explain anything because this time, she wouldn't be wrong if she scolded me. I was the one who put the guard down, and she rightfully deserved an explanation.

I apologized to her and asked her to talk the next morning as Dad and Lilac were asleep.

Did I not read between the lines? Was I wrong to have thought that this could have actually led to something? Was this what he wanted from the start, and I never realised? Something had been off and being utterly pissed, he owed me an explanation. I was sure that he might have gotten the wrong idea, and I really wanted to take things slow so we could talk about it and speak out about our differences.

The next day, I went to the university and could not find him anywhere. I even asked my friends if they had spoken with him. I tried calling, but he would cut my calls every time. This was extremely worrying to me. Was he offended by what I had done? The following day, I tried reaching out to him but failed again. I asked his friends again, and they did meet him that day! This made me even more anxious because nobody responded to me clearly! He would attend all the classes, but then how was I the only one who couldn't find him anywhere? Why was he avoiding me!?

I couldn't understand what was happening to me... After about 2 weeks, I went to his classroom on the 7th floor where he took me, just before recess.

I couldn't believe what I saw!

He was right there, with another girl with a similar headband that he gave me... My heart began aching, and I left the place crying miserably...

As my eyes were blurred with clouds of tears, my vision of the scenario was getting clearer. Reality hit me that I was just a victim of his predatory tendencies, and sadly, not the only one at that! And when he realised that there wasn't much that he could get from me, he ghosted. He was deliberate in avoiding me...

I wasn't the one who transmitted unclear advances; he was the one who hoped to reciprocate his sexual intents upon me, and he felt that since I did not object to him kissing me the first time during the concert, he could very well take the benefit of that and move as ahead as to grab me physically.

Like a fool, I wanted something more emotionally and romantically investing, and stupidly enough, I thought that I would get the same feelings from him. For days, I wouldn't sleep. I would get visuals of the incident. The mere thought of being so naïve and unarmed made me hate my sense of judgment...

I would cry in the shower for hours in the hope that all his foul traces and memories would wear off my body. As a few months passed by, I felt the need to forget this arc from my life forever and pretend as though it never even happened. I made myself completely unapproachable to people again, including my family. Cause I knew that they wouldn't understand me either.

I don't think there's anything left in this entire world that can make me hate men anymore, or so I thought until I met Hadden.

One of the greatest conflicts that I have faced over the years has been that on the one hand was my Father, who was willing to take his own life because he was sure of not being able to bear the pain of losing whom he loved ever-so-deeply, and then there are these people that I encountered in my life, who would use the trust of somebody for something so trivial and short-lived; something that could scar the victim for as long as they can breathe... It has ever since been this unearthly dichotomy of sorts for me that I have to live through and also pretend as though it never happened.

I finally doze off to sleep after the most horrifying day of my entire existence, waiting to be woken up for another painfully long day of labour, knowing fully well that I will never be able to talk about all this with anybody, not even my newly made friends at the dungeon...

CHAPTER 7
THE FEAST

11 months later…

All the horrors now have become part and parcel of our lives. All the other men here do not ever get to touch any of the girls; the uncalled violence from the starting days has terminated entirely. Pleasure in this place for anybody but him is a sin of the highest regard, making him the greatest hypocrite known to mankind, and we all here are his slaves of flesh and desire. Using his powers, he gets his desires fulfilled and then dares to say that he is just on the receiving side of things. For him, he has never touched a woman because that would be 'ungodly of him,' which makes me laugh at him and his delusions even more...

I dream about reuniting with my family every single day, but there's a part of me that has lost hope of returning to my previous life. People in the outside world may have forgotten us by now, but I am determined to go back to my parents and make a new bond with them. They need to know I was their child; I have no idea how I am going to do all this; they may even turn me in for pestering; I'll have to figure it out. They need to know about me...

Besides, the only way out is inside the depths of this place; I need to know everything about Hadden and this place to escape. I have Hadden in my confidence; I need to know how I can break his spell! There must be a way! Anyway, till then, it's only legitimate to do what he commands. That's going to be the only way I'll be alive here. I am never going to waste my life here, crying about affliction.

I am staring at the cell's ceiling as I think all this to myself. I must get up to get dressed before Rojan starts yelling in our faces again.

We proceed to the hall and sit back in our places to begin with the work. Hadden walks in before daybreak to supervise the progress, taking a round of the entire place. While crossing the aisle, he passes me a glance. I get completely annoyed by it but give him back an unpleasant smile. He makes his investigations and then goes back to sit on his throne.

I get chills up my spine and walk towards him hurriedly. He looks at me and smiles again. He is happier than usual today. I sit on his lap and pull my hair to one side, leaning towards him as he sniffs on my neck.

I overheard Souvik whispering to Rojan that all the money from last month's trade had been received by the clients. The clients were happy with the shipment, which increases the chances of expanding our business with them five-fold for the next consignment.

I turned to see Hadden's face as he slid it onto my chest. For the very first time, I have seen him smile. This must be really happy, as his ambitions of conquering the world are a step closer now. He called in for wine for everybody as I was still sitting on his lap, with one side of my chest shoved over his mouth, and Hadden was sucking it patiently like a baby. He paused for a second to raise a toast to everyone for their work. And to his command, everyone's face was overjoyed for his victory and triumph. He declared the day for enjoying and feasting, instructing Malav to arrange for food.

He turned back again towards me to suck my chest.

Souvik saw the perfect opportunity, he came near him and whispered in his ears, seeking permission, "Lord, my brothers and I have worked hard for months to finish this consignment. Would you permit us to ask for something?"

Hadden was indeed in his happiest of moods.

"Go on, Souvik! You have been my most faithful!" he exclaimed.

"We were wondering if we could also enjoy this eve with the girls ..." he dared to ask. The rest of the men behind him listened eagerly.

...

"You MAY!!!!" he screamed, and simultaneously four girls, Thalia, Sunashi, Nina, and Beau, followed them.

We could suddenly hear music playing in our heads, and everyone started dancing again...

"Stop!." Hadden pushed me to the side and stood up from his throne. Everyone paused to see him, at his glaring eyes. "Make sure not to impregnate any of my girls, or I'll kill you that very instant!"

He jumped back to sit and pulled me onto himself as everyone started dancing again...

It was a joyous occasion with real cooked food coming in, a variety of fruits, lots of bread and wine. After about an hour of everyone chuckling around, Hadden turned towards me, leaning both of us at the throne, looking into my eyes... as my hands proceeded towards his lower abdomen. I looked around and felt that the rest of the people had started departing from the hall, leaving behind the two of us, the four men and their escorts for the night. They had laid down on the ground as we leaned against the throne. I could feel that the girls were just mirroring my actions, giving Hadden control of the pleasures of his men as well.

He still had his lower apparel on, so I jumped over on top of him and started moving slowly while the music was still on in our heads. I bent down, kissing all over his chest, while he had a constant gaze at whatever I was doing. His eyes carefully traced all of my moves, making it look like he wasn't the one controlling it at all. Malav started making noises as he hadn't experienced a thing like that before but was ever so desperate for it.

Although it had been months now that we were engaged as being his slaves, there was just something about all this that we never grew. I was just as disgusted by the thought that someone could be so filthy to even think about doing a thing as this just to gain control over someone and their body because they are unable to escape from your well-laid traps...

...

"AVIVE DIED!" Giavanna came running and screamed.

Break –Free

Everyone turned and rushed towards her cell in the very instant.

Her room was filled with splashing rains of blood. There was a text smudged with blood on the wall, 'I'D RATHER BE DEAD THAN BE YOUR SLAVE...'

As everyone was leaving the hall, she had taken one of the blades from there and slit her neck and wrist.

Ironically, it was at that moment, we all realised that we could also free ourselves from Hadden...

By killing ourselves...

We recalled how she had been telling us how traumatising it had been for her even to breathe here, and her sexual encounters every day, at the age of seven years by someone very close to the family, and all the things Hadden made her do would constantly remind her of that; after all the years of trying so hard to forget about it and move ahead.

We then saw various other marks on her body as well, where she had attempted to end her life even before.

I saw Hadden's eyes, and for the first time, there was a real sense of shock in them. I stood next to him, holding his hand, and in a flash, I could read his mind. Scanning the past life of Avive...

The Story of Avive

Coming from one of the wealthiest families in the south of Port Bal City, Avive was always a sweet girl, shy about opening up to anybody but very smart at grabbing and understanding things. For her parents, she had been their trophy child, getting medals in various competitions, outshining academically, and being the first in class. Her parents were extremely proud of her, but this eventually led to her having a lot of people who envied her success within her family. Her parents would throw a grand dinner at different resorts for every accomplishment that she would make.

On one occasion, when she had just won the International Math Quiz at the age of seven, their parents threw a dinner with a grand audience, from the General of the State to the CEO of his Father's company, everyone was there. After cutting the cake, everyone was joyous about the celebration and had a gala when one of her cousins, Amiri, who was also a classmate, called her to the opposite side of the main ballroom. As Avive reached there, Amiri punched her in the face, screaming, "What do you think, you are better than everyone? My Mum hates me because of you!!" He said this and ran away.

Avive stood there crying, with a swollen nose, when his Dad and Uncle Alfie saw her and came towards her, running. She complained to him about how he said those things to her and punched her, and he became red with rage.

'How dare he do this to you? I will teach this guy the lesson he needs!' he roared.

He pulled her close to pat her back and insisted she stop crying, but the pain of her broken nose wouldn't let her stop. He took her to the other room and made her sit in the bed as he sat on the floor on his knees.

"Here, I'll tell you a secret if you promise never to tell anyone."

She nodded as she crossed her heart.

Uncle Alfie: "Truthfully, you were born a Princess, Avive, and I am your bodyguard. King Theodore died during the war, and your mother, Queen Abigail, was constantly being attacked by people from other kingdoms. They asked me to find you a safe place. Your Father had been my friend for a long time, and your current parents wanted to start a family. You were an infant, you wouldn't remember anything. But your parents would never tell you this, since they would also be punished by the royal court for putting your life in danger. You mustn't ask them either; you have promised me... but you are my Princess, Avi. A real Princess. This will be

Amiri's last warning, as he has dared to touch you. Can you keep our promise?"

ˌShe nodded again, wiping off her tears.

Uncle Alfie: "Your Highness, Queen Abigail asked me to teach you the rituals of our kingdom, and after you are 18 years old, you will be crowned as the Queen. You are too young now, but you must eventually learn the traditions of the Land."

She was listening to every word he was saying with absolute concentration.

He flashed her his thing and began speaking, 'This is not how to promise in the land; you have to hold this and pull it until The Lord grants him your wishes.' Avive looked at it, totally confused. He asked her to hold it in her hand and convulse it. "You have to jerk it until you receive his blessings. This is done to lock the seal of commitment. If your soul is impure, you won't receive his blessing."

ˌAs he was saying all this, it enlarged.

"See, The Lord knows that you are about to pray to him. Close your eyes, and pray that you will be a good girl to your parents and all the elders."

She closed her eyes and did as he said.

"Keep your eyes closed and hold onto this thing with both hands, pulling it close to yourself. And promise never to tell your Mum about any of this. You can meet me every month, and I will be teaching you the traditions of our land."

She mumbled everything he said and prayed into nothingness rigorously.

Within a few minutes, she felt a drizzling sensation on her face, after which she opened her eyes.

"Very good. You are an amazing Princess. The Queen was right; you are worthy of being her rightful heir."

Avive's face gleamed as she heard this. Not realising what the devil was doing to her.

As promised, she would meet him every week, and he would fulfill his unholy fetishes with this minor, fooling her as being 'the Princess' of someplace that didn't even exist on the face of Earth. He even made her participate in bondage activities to test her 'strength and agility;' this made her extremely overbearing and brutal.

This went on for 8 years, till she was fifteen when one day, her mother saw bruises on her back and enquired. She grew more curious as Avive was being extremely defensive. This enraged her, and she asked her to remove all her clothes. Avive resisted furiously but her Mum figured that she was lying, as such bruises could not be the result of an accident. She pulled the back strings of her top and discovered all the scars on her body.

Her apprehensions suddenly changed to deep motherly concerns as she was shocked to see those marks on Avive's body and began threatening to call the police if she did not tell her where she got those from. Avive kept on lying to save Uncle Alfie and 'their secret.' Her mother was so traumatised to see her like that that she closed all the doors and terrorised her to be on house arrest if she did not tell her the whole truth. Her Father came home that evening and screamed at her, too, but she still wouldn't spill a word.

After two days of constant shouting and crying, she finally spoke.

Avive (screaming): "Why didn't you guys ever tell me that I was the Princess of Paulstor????"
Avive's Mother: "What the hell are you talking about? And what is this horseshit?"
Avive: "I knew you would never tell me because you want me to trap myself in this house with you..."
[His Mum's rage turned to anxiety]
Avive's Mother: "What is all this Avive, please tell me what are you even saying?"
She was afraid her daughter might have schizophrenia. Her throat went dry as she spoke, and she immediately texted her sister to come over with the doctor.
Avive: "I am Avive, Princess of the Kingdom of Paulstor, daughter of King Theodore Dixon and Queen Abigail Dixon."
Avive's Mother: "Who told you all this, my child? I am your mother and we are your parents. I have delivered you after 9 months of caring for you and we have been with you ever since. Please tell me who told you all this?"

Avive (Her voice changing): "I cannot tell you that; otherwise, I will be punished."

Avive's Mother: "Who will punish you? I will not let anyone put even a finger on you." Her mother was in disbelief about what her daughter had gone through.

She bit her lip and uttered nothing.

Her Mum threatened to kill herself if she didn't admit at once, when finally Avive spoke after all this drama, 'Uncle Alfie did!'

Avive's Father: 'What? Where did he come from?'

Avive: 'He told me that you guys had been hiding this secret away from me for all these years...'

She went on to say everything that had happened to her through the years; her mother's limbs began shaking as she could no longer hold herself together, and she got a panic attack, her blood pressure spiking up fatally. It was for her sister, who came at the right time with the doctor as she was taken to the hospital immediately.

She was discharged in 2 days when she sat down with her husband to talk to Avive, pleading with her to tell them everything and why she had never told them anything before. She was told the real truth about how he had been using her through the years to yield his pleasures, giving her serious damages for life.

They filed a report to the police where she had to tell him everything again, and she was asked to show all the marks and bruises on her body. The juvenile court made up the case against him. She could read by everyone's faces and reactions that she had gotten herself and her parents into some serious trouble, who were brutally scolded by everyone for not looking after her all these years.

As for Uncle Alfie, he was put behind bars back then, with a punishment of 10 years in prison. It took a good 6 months to get the court's verdict, but Avive's parents left no room for error in getting that monster the real taste of his actions.

She was taken to the therapist, and continues to visit her through the years; it had been 8 years since she came here...

For Avive, hell was a safer place to live than Earth...

CHAPTER 8
SELF-DESTRUCT

I just couldn't understand. Last night, I had this strange feeling where I could actually see what Hadden was seeing through us, and according to what he had said a year ago, he had an eye on us since the very beginning; maybe that wasn't true after all. He did not know about this part of Avive's life. And for once, I saw him shed a tear at the loss of one of our most precious. But the strangest thing still remains, that we had a connection yesterday. How did that even happen?

I went to the girls, and we sobbed all night. We knew for sure that this was the only time that we could cry freely because we'd have to go back to work again the next morning, or else Hadden would force us to come there anyway!

I told them how I saw Hadden crying after her demise, too. Avive was the first person there who ever committed suicide; the rest of the people would just be sold off to different places. Nobody knew what happened to them after that, but a thing like this never happened. Hadden, through the years, had always felt that he could control everything and everyone around him, when in reality, he could only make people weak and powerless; he could not take their WILL to NOT live away.

It was supposed to be Sunashi's turn that day to be Hadden's mistress, she was fearfully uninterested to go, but she was also fully aware that none of that really mattered to Hadden.

We were in the main hall when we saw Rojan and the men take Avive's body away to clean up the place. Akia began crying looking at her; we all had been trying to hold back our tears but could no longer... We made sure not to be loud, as Hadden's men would come in any time and harm us.

Akia: "Living each day in this place is becoming more and more like torture. We need to do something to end this suffering."

Giavanna: "You're right. We cannot just go on living like this. It was indeed bold of Avive to have taken such a step..."

Sunashi: "But don't you think this called for more trouble for us? Hadden will now be more careful and keep a sharp eye on all of us. I am certain that his pride has overcome him, but this would require him to take better care of his 'stock.' We all really are just assets for him, and he wouldn't just afford to let any more of us go without generating his profits."

Giavanna: "What do we do then? Live in this torment? We need to break out from this place."
Akia: "Avive did the right thing, and trust me, no one else could really do what she did."
Malav heard her and came towards us with his men; he had a fierce look on his face., and smashed Akia's face.
Malav: "Sunashi, Lord does not seem to be in the right mood today. He wouldn't need you escorting him today."

They shoved us with the eating pills and left.

As all the girls were talking, I couldn't help but think about how Avive had lived all her life and how terrible life had been for her throughout. I did not tell these people any of this; they were already troubled by her suicide... But by whatever I had ever known about her, I was glad she took this step; she had suffered enough. Hadden had also asked Sunashi not to come; I'm sure that he is equally disturbed after knowing about Avive's past. But what also surprises me is that I mind-read him.

Can I use it to my benefit and see if he has really obliviated our families and they are no longer searching for us? He mustn't ever know this, or I'll be dead at his hands.

A certain lightening ran through my body, and I stood up...

I understood at once that it was him. I walked up to his room, and there he stood, looking out the window.

Hadden: "Oh! Mauve. Please come. I'm happy to see you."

I stood there silent. His words almost felt like a joke I was supposed to laugh at. I walked and sat on the couch.

Hadden: "I have never felt so weak, this feeling of losing. Throughout my life, I have only experienced success, but this incident clearly indicated that I was getting older. I wanted to be immortal and be the most powerful man alive! I never hoped to meet this roadblock, and now I don't feel like I'm capable."

(I heard him say all this and just nodded.)

Hadden: "You don't just have to shake your head, Mauve. You are different from the other girls for me. I need you. Every King needs a Queen."

(My eyes blew out as I heard this. I couldn't believe what he said. I had never spoken a word in front of him...)

Hadden: "Please say something. I need you to say something. I can make you my Queen; you'll be my only mistress then, and we'll make the largest kingdom together. I have felt a deep connection between us. Tell me, did you feel it, too?"

Not an ounce of my body moved after he asked me this question, there was absolute silence...

Hadden's expression suddenly changed as a flash turned his eyes blue and spine straight. This was the sensation we would get when he would command us. He stood up and ran towards our dormitory. I religiously followed him until we reached the lady's lavatory.

We could not believe what we saw in front of our eyes; there were corpses in front of us with blood splashed all over the place. I couldn't believe my eyes as I fell on the floor, to see my only friends here, with text over the wall behind them, 'ROT IN HELL.'

My heart began pounding rapidly, and I couldn't breathe. I did not know what to do as I ran to a corner, puking. I tried rubbing my back, I could see blood spills coming out from my mouth, and my head began spinning.

Avive, and now Giavanna, Akia, Astra, Prisca and Sunashi, they all had left me... Left me here alone with this man Hadden, who had now asked me to be his permanent mistress. The thought gave shivers to my body, and I began losing consciousness and fainted...

* * *

Flashback: (After Mauve's Exit)

[Akia and Prisca had a radical stance at Avive's choice of ending her life; she had become a role model for them. Giavanna and Astra were too young to form unbiased opinions. Sunashi strongly opposed it, saying that this place would now be an even bigger danger to their lives]

After I left...

Sunashi: "Hadden seems to be really fond of Mauve. Good thing that he wouldn't be a threat to her now. It was my turn today, but he called her instead."

Astra: "But he should understand what we are going through after Avive's suicide."

Akia: "Suicide? Do you guys really think she committed suicide? She has brutally been murdered by Hadden and his pact of no-brains. Tell me one thing : are any of us really alive here? We all are physically dead and are acting as parts of a machine, that's it!"

Prisca: "You're right. She had been murdered. And we all here, too, are pigs for slaughter."

Astra: "We need justice for Avive!"

Sunashi: "Oh Great! Do you even hear yourself? You guys think that's so easy. Why don't you understand that Hadden would now keep a closer eye on us? You all are kids, brainless and impressionable."

Prisca: "Watch your mouth, Sunashi. Don't you dare speak ill about any of us."

[Astra ran to the washroom, sensing all the commotion.]

Giavanna: "Look at what you guys have done. We just can't be each other's enemies in this whole scenario. We have no one else but each other; we need to look out for each other and not fight! We have already lost one of our most loyal. And Hadden's growing fondness for Mauve tells me that we have good reasons to be on our toes. Nothing's going to happen to her, but we cannot say that about ourselves for sure."

Sunashi: "Yeah, they'll sell us off the moment they see a scar deep enough off our body, which they gave us in the first place, and we will no longer be useful to them."

As she says this, Giavanna comes forward, shaking to show a deep slash mark on her back.

Giavanna: (crying) I don't know what to do; I never thought I'd have to show this to you guys, but there's no way I can hide this anymore, and surely, he'll know this very soon.

Back in the washroom, Astra felt so pathetic about everything that had happened the entire day that she sat on the floor, weeping. Suddenly, she lost breath and began puking. She was spilling blood from her mouth, growing miserable with every second. She started manically slapping herself and hitting her head on the wall till her head swelled up. She couldn't bear the pain of her reality, which she tried to nullify with physical pain.

Akia heard the thumping sound and ran towards the lady's room to see Astra. The rest of the girls followed. All of them were devastated to see Astra screaming and spilling blood all over. They all began crying, seeing the helplessness of their circumstances, and broke out. None of them wanted to bear the horrors of being left alone in the dungeon; they picked up everything that was lying around them to hit themselves, leading to mass self-destruction. Akia cut her wrist deep and scribbled in bold on the wall. They paused at last to hold each other's hand for one last time, and within 10 minutes, all of them died...

* * *

Cut to Hadden's eyes burning with flames of rage and hatred.

He asked Malav to set their bodies on fire.

He completely lost control of his temper and stormed off to his room, pushing Rojan's face into the wall as he stood in the hallway.

My sorrows saw no end to whatever had happened this very day. I dared to touch my girls with grief. Malav, soon after, returned with matchsticks and flammables, and I ran towards my room.

The girls literally left me on my own.

Hadden immediately called for me. But my anger repelled his psychic powers and I was too stubborn to move.

He came to my room and dragged me by my head from there.

'How are you defying my commands? I am your Lord!' he screamed at the top of his lungs. 'You will stay with me now!'

He called Souvik and asked him to wrap up all my stuff and move them to his room.

I professed Hadden to let me mourn peacefully that night and not even dare to command me to touch him. He was infuriated at first, but his eyes agreed with helplessness, he touched my hands and I saw through him everything that happened with the girls after I had left.

When Astra ran puking.

She was pregnant...

(There was a death of a silence)

Hadden impregnated her when she was his mistress.

I looked at Hadden with disbelief since she was just sixteen.

This day was growing worse by every second... Hadden bowed down to me, apologising for what he had done... I was still in distrust and repudiation...

He wanted me to see through him, and he knew that I could read his mind. He was letting me do it, being too cowardly to admit!

For three days, I didn't move from one place and just kept crying at the happenings of the past few days. and how I lost whom I thought would be with me through the misery. I did not even eat anything. Hadden wouldn't force food in my mouth like he did earlier. My body was worsening, too, with my bones popping out of my skin.

I desperately wished I could be with the girls when they were committing suicide because now Hadden wouldn't leave me for a moment.

He was too scared to let me go, and he knew that all his stock would do that to themselves one day, so he better keep an eye on them all the time, too.

One day I overheard him talking to Rojan, asking him to go along with the rest, for the next hunt season. They weren't able to meet their projected deal requirements, with a lesser number of working hands.

He would come back to the room every day and would watch me lie in the same position, and the same condition. He would feel sorry for me but wouldn't force me onto anything. He grew equally powerless, looking at the condition I had made for myself.

After five days of constant mourning, he held me up and made me sit next to him. He held my hand and placed it on his left chest, making me sense his heartbeat.

It was in this flash that I had visions of how he was able to control us. The different food pills they had been giving us all along wired us to him as the only central nervous system, taking away the power to make decisions for us! Since I had not been feeding myself out of grief, he had lost total control over my body...

This potion was among the darkest of arts prohibited to be practised on a living being. He was no God, just a disillusioned showman, running this whole animal poaching racket, using humans as slaves to work for him and give him the pleasure he would be deprived of in his life!

All this meant that...

I could actually escape...

End of Part 1.

Disclaimer: Reader's Discretion

This book is not meant for a universal audience, as there are certain sensitive subjects explored, which include:

1. Mental Health: Anxiety and Panic Attack
2. Nudity
3. Physical Assault
4. Sexual Violence
5. Suicide

Characters

1. **Mauve** - The Protagonist
2. **Lilac (Affectionately called Lil'ass)** - Mauve's sister
3. **Avive** - Prison mate and friend
4. **Elisa Iodice** - Mauve's childhood best friend
5. **Prisca** - Mauve's Prison mate and friend
6. **Sunashi** - Prison mate
7. **Akia** - Prison mate
8. **Astra** - Prison mate
9. **Giavanna** - Prison mate
10. **Hadden** - The Antagonist
11. **Souvik** - Cult member / Conductor
12. **Rojan** - Cult member / Bus Driver

13. **Raven** - Cult member
14. **Malav** - Cult member
15. **Uncle Alfie** - Avive's Uncle
16. **Sharya** - Lilac's bitch friend
17. **Enzo Iodice** - Elisa's brother
18. **Rian** - Cute (not really) guy from college
19. **Thalia** - Prison mate
20. **Nina** - Prison mate
21. **Beau** - Prison mate
22. **Amiri** - Avive's Cousin

Special Thanks

Apart from my parents who deserve a separate section of acknowledgement, I would also like to thank my brother, Vivek Naik (who generally doesn't talk to anyone) for greatly shaping my childhood and being my only mirror of morality.

My siblings, who have shown immense support in every stage of life, and have also contributed by giving just the right advice at the right time! Harry Naik, Nikita Das, Evleena Naik, Hitesh Jerai, Priyanka Pragya and Anmol Sinku mean nothing less than the world to me!

Mr Guru Charan Naik, Mrs Neelkamal Naik, Mrs Kavita Sinku, Mr Birendra Sinku, my beloved late Ms Golanti Naik, late Mr Sarat Chandra Naik, and late Mrs Parbati Naik, who have taken great care of me and blessed my very being from the moment that I breathed on the surface of Earth.

My amazing friend circle has been with me through thick and thin, despite the hardships that came along the way, making my belief in human connections stronger!

My hype gang of school friends and precious pieces of heart, Arpita, Aastha, Sana, Gloriana, Vaibhavi and Aakanksha. Literal Bros for life; Saket, Rajat, Abhishek, Kalash and Aadi. And my lovely juniors Nimish and Onkar.

My friends-turned-sisters Apoorva, Shreya and Monali.

My college friends are Aditi, Nandu, Namrata, Madhumita, and Sakshi. My greatest support and friendly advisor Krishna. My super helpful and fun seniors Harsh sir and Amit sir!

Cannot speak enough about these people who have been with me through ups and downs and still stand strong! Lots of friendships and meaningful connections have been with me throughout my life, some gave me peace and happiness, and the rest have given me the greatest lessons to cherish and treasure forever!

Beyond anything else, a huge shoutout to my roots in the suburbs of Bhilai (Chhattisgarh) for being my comfort place! I would despise the whole city for not being 'cool' enough back in childhood, but I crave going back there more than ever now The countless number of memories the place has given me, every street of sector-10 has a story hidden for me, and I owe my everything to this place for being so nice to me, in a bittersweet way!

Note From The Author

The Journey of this novel:

The story came into being as the consequence of a dream I had in 2021 (during the second wave of COVID-19) and wasn't willing to let go of. It was one of those dreams that I did not want to forget and one of my closest friends gave me the idea to write a book on it when I told her about it. This sole statement had been the game-changer for me, and after crossing all the roadblocks/writer's blocks/plot and character developments, I finally determined to finish this book after 3 years and also publish it! It has taken me a lot of spine and confidence to get where I am! The world had changed my perspective on the book. I am glad I could achieve what I did, and this has been my greatest motivation, so if there's even a little soul who I have inspired to work towards their dream, I can sleep in peace.

Share your Love

If you have arrived at this part of the book, I have the deepest gratitude for you and I would love to know your most candid and genuine thoughts about it to improve the story!

Average Indian Whore is my 2nd stand-alone book (an exclusive abstract at the end of the book)

I am open to taking in personal stories and memoirs from individuals who want their stories to be presented to the world as both; a biography or a spiced-up piece of fiction.

Do write to me at - dv.yourssincerely@gmail.com

If you like my book, leave a review of the book on the Amazon link of 'Telekinesis: Vol. 1 Victims of His Head by Devleena Naik' / Flipkart or on Goodreads, feel free to tag or follow me on Instagram for more updates for my upcoming novel 'Average Indian Whore' on - @devleenanaik and @dv_purplesun.

You can also order a customized Author's signed-copy Gift Box for your loved ones. Just email me on dv.yourssincerely@gmail.com the person you want to send this gift to!

An exclusive extract from Devleena Naik's
upcoming novel

Average Indian Whore

The Story of Obsessive Delusion

Follow @dv_purplesun for more updates

"It's been raining cats and dogs for the past one hour and I had just come to get the groceries on my bike. I try my hardest to escape the heavy pouring rain, but the raindrops are blinding my eyes. There's no choice but to wait out here in the rain! I park at a shop's corner to remove my glasses, still standing by for the rain to stop, but my myopic eyes blur my vision over again, I take off my specs to wipe them off clean and as I wear them back again, I sense something unnervingly suspicious... My fears grow loud as I look around... I bawl myself all over in a hasty manner, almost feeling all my breaths, I see no one...

I understand at once.

It's him.

It could be nobody else but him.

He who breathes in my shadows,

Follows me like the breeze,

Guards me like a canine...

Wherever I go, whatever I do, he's right there waiting for me...

He walks as I walk, he stops as I halt. His footprints follow me everywhere...

My footsteps have lost their unique sound, they have become one with his...

Weirdly enough, it feels comfortably secure that I am never really alone, but the rest of the time, it feels just as haunting, because I Am Never Alone.

He is always there...

But he never talks, so what's the whole point of being around?

You could have just been a friend? But that way, you were pretty self-aware that you knew you were never worth me, so of all the times you asked, I turned you down... Warned you to never even try to get close to me, begged your friends to talk some sense into you, and cried before your blood to spare me my life, but then you turned to these petty ways, sniffing all my steps. Fact-checking every human I ever laid my eyes on. Thinking I'd never notice. But I have given up, given up yelling at you to be by your limits, 'cause you have none, none for me for the least!

I used to fancy you having a little more self-worth, but I guess, we're both way past that realization. Heaven may know what you achieve by doing all this!

My friends called you 'Delusional', but I told them that you no longer even feel like a stalker, you are now, unofficially my guard dog! Not gonna lie, that one time I put my arm on Ron, I sensed you burning, enjoyed it even. Thinking like a juvenile, that it would make you never wanna see me again. Instead, you sent Ron's chats with his girlfriend to his mother, who then made sure Ron never got close to any girl...

The raindrops have lowered, I take my bicycle again and rush out, and the very moment, I see him come out from behind the other shop, taking his bicycle. I smiled to myself and left...